PROPERTY OF:

TEXACO